PAW PATROL™: ALL STAR PUPS
A CENTUM BOOK 9781912707416
Published in Great Britain by Centum Books Ltd
First published 2018
This edition published 2021
3 5 7 9 10 8 6 4 2

Centum Books Ltd, 20 Devon Square, Newton Abbot, Devon TQ12 2HR, UK
9/10 Fenian St, Dublin 2, D02 RX24, Ireland
books@centumbooksltd.co.uk
CENTUM BOOKS Limited Reg. No. 07641486

A CIP catalogue record for this book is
available from the British Library

Printed in Great Britain

ALL STAR PUPS

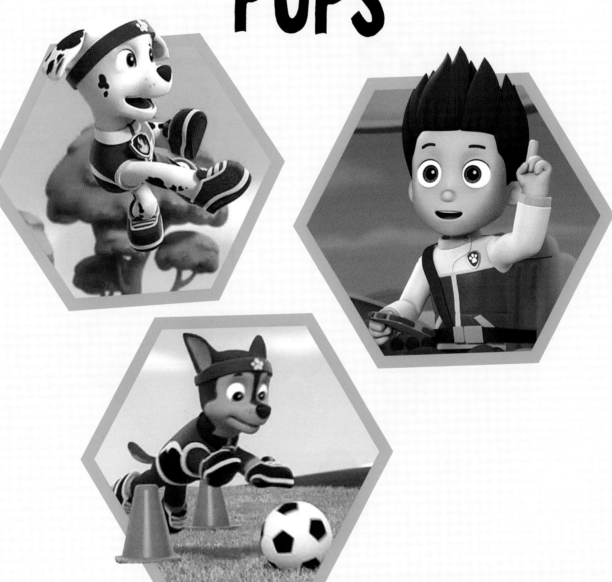

centum

STARRING ...

EVEREST

MARSHALL

RAIMUNDO

SKYE

CHASE

RYDER

RUBBLE

The PAW Patrol is outside practising for a special charity sports day. The pups will compete against Mandy the monkey and her family to raise money for a new big top for the circus.

Chase kicks the ball to Skye ...

who passes it to Marshall ...

who leaps to catch it ...

but falls in a heap!

BUMP!

Raimundo the circus master calls Ryder on the PupPad. He's on his way to Adventure Bay with the monkeys.

"Hi Ryder," says Raimundo. "My amazing monkey athletes and I are almost there."

Ryder rounds up the pups.

"Okay pups, let's get the equipment to the sports field," says Ryder. "Let the games begin!"

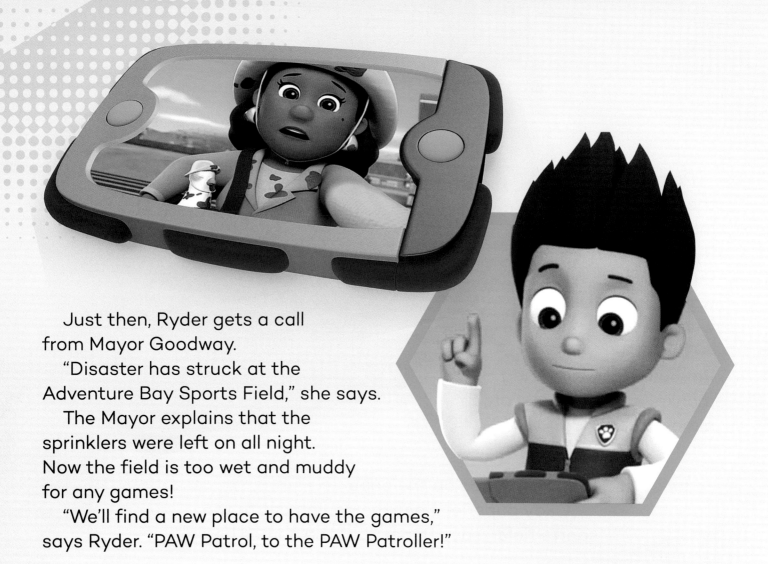

Just then, Ryder gets a call from Mayor Goodway.

"Disaster has struck at the Adventure Bay Sports Field," she says.

The Mayor explains that the sprinklers were left on all night. Now the field is too wet and muddy for any games!

"We'll find a new place to have the games," says Ryder. "PAW Patrol, to the PAW Patroller!"

Inside the PAW Patroller, Ryder tells the pups about the muddy field.
"We'll have to move the games somewhere else," Ryder says. "Like...."
"Farmer Al's!" the pups cheer together. Ryder and the pups call
their farmer friend.
"My sheep and I would be glad to lend you our pasture for the games,"
says Farmer Al.

"The only problem is the field. It's full of grass and rocks," warns Al.

"No problem. Herd the sheep safely into the barn and we'll take care of the rest," Ryder says.

"Glad to oblige," nods Al.

"Baaaa!" one of his sheep chips in.

Ryder calls up the pups for the job:
    "Rubble, we need your construction rig to clear the field and dig the track. Marshall, you can use your paint cannons to mark the running lanes."
    "Rubble on the double," says Rubble.
    "I'm fired up," adds Marshall.

Soon Rubble, Marshall and Ryder are on their way towards Al's Farm, followed by the PAW Patroller. PAW Patrol is on a roll! Nothing must get in the way of raising money for the new big top.

As soon as the crew reach the stony field Rubble gets straight to work. He starts to clear the ground to make a running track, but it's not easy.

"It's going to take forever to move these stones one-by-one," he warns Ryder.

Ryder comes up with a way to solve the problem. First he calls Raimundo.

"Raimundo, can your monkeys play kickball?" he asks.

"Sure. They can play any ball game," says Raimundo.

"In that case, let's make a kickball field. We can do that much faster," says Ryder.
"I can dig it!" laughs Rubble.

Once the kickball field is ready, it's time for Marshall to paint in the lines.

"Ruff ruff. Paint cannons!" he says and the cannons zoom out of his Pup Pack.

Meanwhile Rocky looks in his recycling truck and finds the perfect tiles to use for bases.

By the time Raimundo and his monkeys arrive everything is set for the charity kickball game. Mayor Goodway and Chickaletta are there to officially start the action.

"Everybody have fun," says the Mayor.

"Let's play ball!" adds an excited Raimundo.

The pups and the monkeys are soon showing their skills.

The monkeys can do circus tricks with the ball.

The pups are great at kicking it hard.

Farmer Al's sheep peep out of the barn and one little lamb decides she'd like to join in, too!

The game is going well but high above them someone else has seen the bouncy red kickball....
Suddenly an eagle swoops down and grabs it in her beak!

"The nerve of that bird, stealing our ball!" cries Mayor Goodway, but there's nothing they can do.

Ryder uses his binoculars to watch where the eagle flies.

"She's gone back to her nest high up on the mountaintop," he says. "Skye, if you could use your copter to distract the eagle Everest could use her grappling hook to climb the mountain and get the ball back."

"Gotta fly," says Skye. "I don't think I've ever played tag with an eagle before."

"Off the trail, Everest won't fail," adds Everest.

"Let's go!" says Ryder, and the three brave friends leap into action.

Everest and Ryder drive to the bottom of the mountain. It's as far as they can go. Now it's up to Everest to climb to the top.

"Okay, Skye. It's time to make the eagle look at you instead of Everest," orders Ryder, and Skye swoops down in her copter.

"Come on eagle.
Try to catch me," she says.
"But don't try too hard.
That beak of yours is BIG!"

"Ruff, ruff. Grappling hook,"
says Everest. She uses it
to make her way up
the mountainside.

When she reaches the nest she gets a surprise.
"There are two little chicks playing with the ball,"
she tells Ryder. "We can't leave them without a toy."
"You're right. Skye, do you have anything in your
copter that will be a good toy for them?" asks Ryder.

"How about my wind-up mouse, Mr Squeakums?" Skye suggests. "I'll miss him but the monkeys need their new big top and I'm sure the chicks will love him."

Everest gently takes the ball from the chicks and drops it down to Ryder. Then Skye gives them Mr Squeakums to play with instead. The chicks are delighted and Skye can see that they will look after him.

Ryder, Skye and Everest speed back to the kickball field, where everyone is waiting.

"Here's the kickball, and it's still bouncy!" says Ryder.

It's Marshall's turn and he does a great kick to win the game. The monkeys don't mind losing to the PAW Patrol. They have collected enough charity money to get a new big top!

"Thank you, Ryder," says Raimundo.

"No problem. Whenever you're in trouble, just yelp for help," says Ryder.

"Ruff, ruff," adds Marshall. "That was a yelp for snack time!"

There are treats for the pups and bananas for the monkeys. Now that's a win-win for everyone!

THE END